CARTOON NETWORK

SCOOBY-DOO!™

Illustrated by Animagination, Inc.
and CaveMan Productions

Written by Emily Thorton Calvo and Joel Zadak

Published by Louis Weber, C.E.O.
Publications International, Ltd.
7373 North Cicero Avenue
Lincolnwood, Illinois 60712

Manufactured in U.S.A.

8 7 6 5 4 3 2 1

ISBN 0-7853-3913-2

Publications International, Ltd.

Welcome to Funland Amusement Park! Kids had fun here, but now Mr. Jenkin's haywire, ghostly robots are up to foul play. Scooby-Doo and his friends are out to capture the ghostly gadgets, but more than one robot is trying to take them for a ride.

Take a look and see if you can find Scooby-Doo and his amusing pals trying to put the fun back in Funland.

Chip Disk
Scooby-Doo Robo
Robo-Ghost
Heavy Metal
Robo-Mop
R2D2B12
Robo-Bobo the Clown
WAX MUSEUM
R & R RAILROAD
DISORIENTED EXPRESS
ROBOT REPAIRS
Tunnel of Love
RUST STOP
CAUTION: MUSHY STUFF AHEAD

FERRIS WHEEL'S DAY OFF
ROLLER DERBY COASTER
FORTUNE TELLING
HOT DOGS
BALL TOSS

While at the Museum of Archaeology, Scooby and friends are chased by a ghastly mummy. The monster wants an ancient coin that's the key to unlocking a priceless treasure. The gang needs help to find the coin before the mummy does.

Help unravel the mystery by finding the gold coin and these other characters that have gotten all "wrapped" up in this mystery:

Gold Coin

Mummy Scooby

Gummy Mummy

Ghostly Gardener

Mr. Volt

Dr. Dig

Chef Mummy-Mia

Siamese Scaredy-Cat

SNACKS
MAN'S EVOLUTION
HOMO-SCOOBUS
HOMO-ERECTUS
HOMO-CRAWLUS
RAGS TO RICHES
FLOATIN' PHARAOH
COOKIES
WRAP
KISS THE COOK
MUMMY DEAREST
DADDIES
MUMMIES FOR DUMMIES
DIG 2000

The ghost of Red Beard and his spooky pirate ship are haunting the sea, and the mystery gang wants to know what's really going on. Through dense fog they find the ship, but where's Red Beard? Zoinks! He pops out of the woodwork—and he's captured Shaggy and Scooby! The ship's creepy crew is hungry, and Red Beard wants Shag and Scoob to make dinner for them.
Find Scooby then help our fearful heroes find the eerie ingredients of Pirate Stew:
Pirate Scooby
Half a Crow's Nest
Pieces of Eight
A Dash of Pepper
Shivered Timbers
A Barrel of Laughs
A Twist of Lime
A Sprinkle of Gun Powder
PUMPKIN PATCH
EYE PATCH
CARROT PATCH
THIS WAY
THAT WAY
ANCHORS AWEIGH
MOVERS & SHAKERS

SPARE TIRES
FINISH
HOOK'S
LINES & SINKERS
CORN:
A BUCK AN EAR
Tastes Like Chicken
Snack Shop
ONE NIGHT
ONLY:
SCURVY
LOST
MARBLES
FOUND
MARBLES

Scooby-Doo and the gang head for the mountains on a ski weekend. After hearing about the Yeti Snow Ghost that's been terrorizing the area, Scooby-Doo and the gang know there's a mystery to solve!
Ice is not the only thing sparkling on these peaks, there are secret jewels the Snow Ghost doesn't want anyone to find. Help the gang find the jewels, catch the monster, alert the sheriff, and try to have some fun on their trip.
Sheriff
Snow Ghost
Snowmobile
White Timberwolf
Ice-Scoob
Ghoul's Jewels
CART BLANCHE
NORTH POLE
SALT
SAW MILL
SNOW ROUTE
NO PARKING WHEN SNOW IS OVER 1000 INCHES!!
SLOW
ICE SCULPTURE CONTEST
SLOW

PEPPER
SNOW TIRES
RESORT TO SKIING
CREEPY SLEEPY LODGE
SANTA SLEPT HERE
FROZEN FOOD COURT
RESERVATIONS
LODGE
SPECIAL: YETTI SPAGETTI
HOG SLED RIDES
SNO GLOBE GIFT SHOP
MELTAWAYS
YETTI PETTYS
BOOKS
MELTAWAYS
SNOW IT ALL
ESKIMO PIE
BLUEBERRY AND APPIE
POLAR ROOT BEER
CLIFF'S CLIFF

It's the Chinese New Year! Scooby-Doo and the gang visit Chinatown to join in the celebration. But soon after the parade starts, the art gallery's Golden Mask mysteriously "floats" away. And jinkies! The Scare Pair has decided now is a good time to spook the streets. With all of the fright and festivities, the gang decides to aid Inspector Fong in unmasking this creepy crime.

Help the Mystery Gang find the Golden Mask and these crazy characters:

The Golden Mask

Inspector Fong

Scare Pair

Rick Shaw

Tai Kwon Do

Yin & Yang

Scooby-Doo Kung Fu

CHOP CLASS
BUSTER CHOPS, INSTRUCTOR
KARATE
103
DOG DAYS
INN
LOW FAT
NEXT SHOW 10
YEAR of the RABBIT
WAREHOUSE
BAIT SHOP
GONE FISHING
FISHERMAN'S WHARF
TITANIC

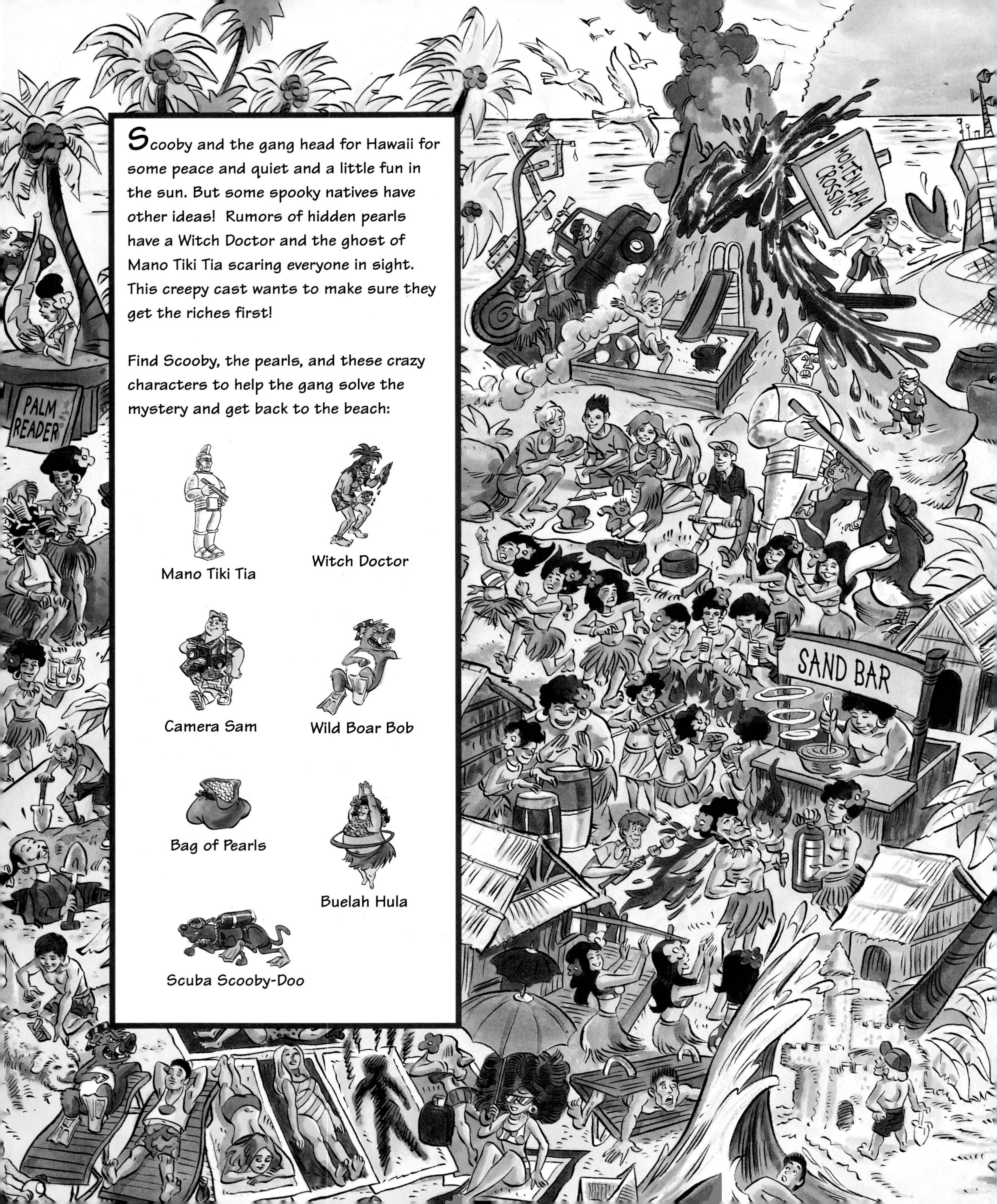

Scooby and the gang head for Hawaii for some peace and quiet and a little fun in the sun. But some spooky natives have other ideas! Rumors of hidden pearls have a Witch Doctor and the ghost of Mano Tiki Tia scaring everyone in sight. This creepy cast wants to make sure they get the riches first!
Find Scooby, the pearls, and these crazy characters to help the gang solve the mystery and get back to the beach:
Mano Tiki Tia
Witch Doctor
Camera Sam
Wild Boar Bob
Bag of Pearls
Buelah Hula
Scuba Scooby-Doo
PALM READER
MOLTEN LAVA CROSSING
SAND BAR

BERMUDA TRIANGLE
KOKOMO SQUARE
BORA BORA CIRCLE
COLD DRINKS
HOT COCOA
LOST ART
1.5
6
HEAD SHRINKING SPECIAL
NO BRAINER
DEAD END
DANGER: KEEP OUT!
LOST AND FOUND
TAKA LEKI
LOST CAT
NATIVE GHOSTS ONLY

Scooby-Doo and the gang visit a castle expecting to get the royal treatment. But a freaky phantom is causing a royal pain. The ghastly ghost is looking for a treasure that has been hidden away. And ghosts are everywhere causing the royal blues.
Explore the castle and see if you can find the treasure chest, the Phantom and some loyal royals.
Queen Bee
Scooby-Duke
King Crab
Silent Knight
Foot Prince
Royal Jewels
Phantom of the Castle
GHOSTS: 9
GOBLINS: 4
BOO-TANICAL GARDENS
BAM-BOO SHOOTS
SNAP DRAGONS
WEEDS
POISON IVY
DEAD CENTER
BURIED HATCHETS
GROUND FLOOR OPPORTUNITY
REALLY DEEP DISH PIZZA
BOO-BERRY PIE

SWEET SCREAMS
NO PETS ALLOWED
HAUNTED CASTLE MAP
BLOOD DONORS WELCOME
POOL HALL
GHOUL HALL
NO BRIDGE PLAYING

Green trees. Peaceful lakes. Roaring campfires. There's nothing like a camping trip to get away from it all. But it seems that an eerie werewolf has gotten Scooby and the gang wrapped up in yet another mystery. The marshmallows and hot dogs will have to wait until the fearless crew gets to the bottom of this hair-raising mystery.

Find the werewolf's treasure map, the creepy werewolf, and these other nutty nature buffs:

- Treasure Map
- Ranger Rickity
- Timber Buck II
- The Werewolf
- A Fox in Socks
- Forest Stump
- Scooby-Doo-BBQ

MINE
GET YOUR OWN
WOLF CROSSING
OLD MILL
BEAR HUGS 50¢
SILAS LONG
MISTER BONE JANGLES
WASH 'N WEARWOLF DYED 1980
THE MYSTERY MACHINE
POISON IVY RELIEF
CONE SWEET CONE
NURSERY
CREEPY CREEK

Go back to Funland Amusement Park and gather all these amusing tools to keep the rides in gear:

____ Screw "driver"
____ Monkey Wrench
____ C-saw
____ Nuts and Bolts
____ "Rock" Hammer
____ "Mask"ing Tape

Go back to the museum to discover these other Egyptian things:

____ Egyptian Stinks
____ Pharaoh's Faucet
____ "Mummies for Dummies"
____ A Pair of Pyramids
____ Cleopatra's Wig
____ Hippo-glyphics
____ A Scroll on a Stroll

Once the police arrive to bring Red Beard and his goons to justice, they will need to recover all the stolen valuables. Go back to the spooky shore to find these precious items:

____ Treasure "Chest"
____ Two "Carrot" Diamond
____ Tennis Bracelet
____ Ivory Tower
____ "Marble" Statue

The gang finds out that there's no business like snow business. Go back to their ski weekend to find these snowy things:

____ A Snow Bunny
____ Iced "T"
____ Ice "Patch"
____ Snow "Suit"
____ Snow Cap
____ A Snow Angel

Go back to Chinatown to watch the parade. Keep your eyes peeled for this menu of crazy cuisine:

____ Bird's Nest Soup
____ Green "T"
____ Egg "Roll"
____ Peeking Duck
____ Moo Shoes
____ Empress Chicken
____ Egg "Drop" Soup

Try to keep your cool under the hot Hawaiian sun. Go back to the sandy beaches to find these "sandy" things:

____ Sand "Bank"
____ Sand Box
____ Sand Castle
____ Sand "Man"
____ Sand Trap
____ Sand Witch

Return to the castle and find all these ghostly characters who are being royal pests:

____ Boo Moon
____ Boo-by Trap
____ Boobeard the Pirate
____ Kanga-boo
____ Cari-boo
____ Boo-tanical Garden

Go back to the camping trip in the woods. Then branch out to find these very unusual trees:

____ Shoe Tree
____ Family Tree
____ Palm Tree
____ Tree-ring Circus
____ Money Tree
____ Fur Tree